FINDING GRACE

A **HIDE AND** SEEK BOOK

WRITTEN BY GRACE AND MOMMY MAGNUSSEN
ILLUSTRATIONS BY ELETTRA CUDIGNOTTO

 FriesenPress

One Printers Way
Altona, MB R0G 0B0
Canada

www.friesenpress.com

ISBN
978-1-03-915599-2 (Hardcover)
978-1-03-915598-5 (Paperback)
978-1-03-915600-5 (eBook)

1. JUVENILE FICTION, FAMILY, PARENTS

Distributed to the trade by The Ingram Book Company

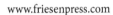
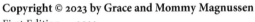
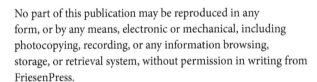

Dedication Page:

This book, and my life, is dedicated to my most precious and undeserving gift, my daughter Grace.

Dear Kids:

This is a hide and seek book!!

Find Grace, 'the princess of light', hiding in each picture.

Sometimes, she is hiding multiple times in a few of the pictures.

She appears a total of 17 times. Can you find them all!?!?

There are also fun activities at the end of the book for kiddos to check out!

The Mother cried on the swings at the park and sang:

I'm gonna stand by your fire
And believe in a higher...power
Bringing my flower,
Home to me

The Mother was looking down, way down.

She was looking at the bottom of the barrel!

The Mother was looking for her Daughter, Grace.

She had already looked at the library; no luck.

She went to the nearby pool; no sign.

The Mother rung the Daddy again and again; no answer.

Her Daughter meant absolutely everything to her.

Everywhere the Mother searched, she made absolutely sure to examine every nook and cranny. She began looking in all the dark places too, including spooky tunnels, and grungy garbage barrels.

Desperate to find Grace, the Mother even fell into the garbage barrel she was looking in!

Twisted and afraid, from the bottom of the barrel, she sang:

I'm gonna stand by your fire
And believe in a higher...power
Bringing my flower,
Home to me

While warming her hands at a campfire,

The Mother called the 1-800- Daughter helpline.

The Mother cried, "PLEASE, HELP ME FIND MY DAUGHTER. I have been looking everywhere for 1,008 hours, including the bottom of barrels!"

"Miss, are you in any danger?" asked the helpline attendant.

"No," lied the Mother anxiously.

The helpline attendant took a moment and briefly looked through the cloud history of the Mother's past few days looking for her daughter.

"I cannot help you, but I can tell you this message...

Stop looking at the bottom of barrels. She is not there for there is no light, only darkness. Grace is bright light, she is not at the bottom of any barrels. LOOK ELSEWHERE!"

At last, she began to feel a hopeful sensation inside. She began planning her journey to the brightest place she could think of; the 'Castle of the Light'. She heard that a very wise King lived there.

But....The Castle of Light was located in the clouds on the tallest mountain.

Many did not dare to venture to the Castle. Quicksand, a jungle full of snakes, a fire-breathing dragon, and a shark infested moat, are just a few of the things guarding the castle. Despite the hard road ahead, the Mother laid underneath the stars, and with a smile, she sang:

> I'm gonna stand by your fire
> And believe in a higher...power
> Bringing my flower,
> Home to me

The next morning, the Mother began her quest to 'The Castle of Light'. But... she had so many more obstacles to overcome.

The Mother danced through quicksand so she would NOT sink.

She vaulted over tall stones so she would NOT catch fire.

She swung on tree vines so she would NOT be bit by snakes.

She even made friends with the snakes, who to her delight, linked together when the tree vines ran out.

As nighttime fell, she started to get scared. Luckily, she met with a colorful dragon and asked for help to make it through the spooky forest. The dragon, with his blaze of fire, lit up the forest so she could find her way.

Next, she had to climb a huge mountain. She slipped! BUT... a magical life-sized butterfly lifted her up to safety.

The final step to reach 'The Castle of Light' was to cross the shark infested moat. To do this she created a shark fin for her back so she would blend in. She also befriended yet another friendly creature, the narwhal.

The next day, after a long and exhausting journey, the Mother finally arrived at the 'Castle of Light'.

Before knocking on the door, she eagerly sang:

> I'm gonna stand by your fire
> And believe in a higher...
> Bringing my flower,
> Home to me

She went to knock and before she could, the King appeared and said, "Well, well, well, it took you long enough to find the light, didn't it my dear? Your Daughter, Grace, was discovered to be a Princess of Light." The King continued, "I have taken her to live as Royalty with us in the 'Castle of Light'."

The Mother fell to her knees and **BEGGED** to see her Daughter.

The King led the Mother inside and said, "To prove Grace, the Princess of Light, belongs with you, you must answer one riddle."

The King took a BIG breath in, and a BIG breath out, and another BIG breath in, and then on the next breath out... a massive barrel appeared. The King then asked the riddle.

"What do you put in a barrel to make it <u>lighter</u>?

The Mother thought for a minute. She had looked at the bottom of plenty of barrels.

Everything inside had made it heavier, except one thing. There was a hole in the last barrel she had seen.

Not only would the hole in the barrel make it physically lighter, she also noticed how it allowed the light in, thus making it lighter in that aspect as well!

The Mother replied with a triumphant smile, "A hole makes a barrel lighter. By putting a hole in a barrel, you remove some darkness and let in some light. This makes the barrel lighter!

The King was impressed and brought forth, Grace, Princess of Light.

The Mother cried and sang:

I'm gonna stand by your fire
And believe in a higher...power
Bringing my flower,
Home to me

The Mother and Daughter hugged, kissed and went home to cuddle!

The End.

Activity Pages

Hey kids, spot the ten differences in the pictures below! One is already done as an example for you. ☺

Hey kids, color in the pictures below!

Hey kids, can you find the following items in the picture below?

**Find: 1 Sun 1 Castle 1 Tree 1 Rainbow
3 Birds 5 Hearts 1 Door 1 Smile**

Hey kids, looking at the picture below, can you answer the following questions?

What are the colors of the rainbow?
How many hearts are in this picture?
Who do you love?
Who loves you?

About the Incredible Illustrator: (she/her)

Elettra Cudignotto, a.k.a. Elettra, is from Vicenza, Italy and was born in 1990. In 2012 she graduated with a degree in Visual Arts and in 2014 obtained a degree in Economics and Management of Arts. She began work as a freelance illustrator in 2015 and this remains her full time, beloved work - which surprises her day by day! You can find out more about Elettra by visiting her website, www.elettracudignotto.com or locating her on Instagram @elettraillustration.
Elettra can also be reached via email at the following address: elettra90@gmail.com

About the real Princess of Light: 👧

Grace is 8 years old and is currently in Grade 3 at a French Catholic School. Grace loves art, singing, dancing, and of course her baby Brother! Grace was the inspiration for this book as she, like all children, radiates her positive energy and reminds us to look on the brighter side of our challenges. Grace was not only the inspiration for this book, but she also drew concept drawings for the Illustrator, Elettra, to use as a guide. Grace also drew the last two activity pages in this book as well! Grace has a beautiful kind heart and is always seeking to help others. Grace brings light and love into the world, and is gifted at finding the silver linings in challenging times, and thus gained herself the title of, "the Princess of Light".☀

About the Ambitious Author: (ze/ zir)

Rhea Magnussen (A.K.A "Mommy Magnussen") is from Humboldt, Saskatchewan. Rhea graduated from the University of Saskatchewan with a degree in accounting and then obtained a CPA designation. Rhea currently has a modest tax business that ze runs during tax season. Rhea also recently fulfilled a life-long dream as she opened up a gymnastics club in Clavet, called Finding Grace Gymnastics Club. Along with writing, Rhea fills zir time with coaching gymnastics and of course, the love of zir life, zir daughter, Grace. Rhea wrote this book in response to a period of extreme hardship in life where ze was separated from zir daughter, and has used its process as a healing journey. The main message of the book of "renewing your mind from darkness to light" tackles the issue of depression and how sometimes it can be all too easy to take for granted our most precious gift- our children.

Rhea is currently back at the University of Saskatchewan- this time studying psychology, with the master plan of becoming a child counsellor. Rhea plans to continue writing and using real life experiences and her newfound love for psychology to develop a children's book series that tackles difficult mental health topics. Her next book is based on her Father's life in Foster Care and is called "Master Ricki". Rhea finds it extremely important to communicate with kids about difficult topics that they may or may not have been exposed to. Rhea uses a magical world and has many intertwined metaphors in the book "Finding Grace", to discuss the topic of depression and family separation in a way children can understand. Children can be exposed to divorce and a variety of mental health issues. It is time we start talking about these challenges to our kids!

Rhea would like to thank zir family for their endless support and encouragement.

Rhea identifies as non-binary and uses the pronouns ze/zir.

This Book Belongs To Superstar _____

Thank you for your supporting a new Saskatchewan Author! A portion of all proceeds are donated to local Not for Profit organizations supporting families and their mental health. This book is a reminder of our most precious gifts in life; our children!

CPSIA information can be obtained
at www.ICGtesting.com
Printed in the USA
JSHW071044180723
44883JS00005B/144

9 781039 155985